For Rafe and Hugo: may you always dare to fail ~ S. S.

For D.D. ~ F. I.

tiger tales

5 River Road, Suite 128, Wilton, CT 06897
Published in the United States 2023
by Little Tiger Press Limited
Text by Stephanie Stansbie
Text copyright © 2023, Little Tiger Press Limited
Illustrations copyright © 2023, Frances Ives
ISBN-13: 978-1-6643-0033-0
ISBN-10: 1-6643-0033-3
Printed in China
LIO/1400/0436/0423
2 4 6 8 10 9 7 5 3 1

www.tigertalesbooks.com

The Owl who Dared

by Stephanie Stansbie

Illustrated by Frances Ives

tiger tales

"Is it time to wake up?" said a little owl one night.

"It is," said his mom. "The sun has begun to fade."

"I still have sleep in my head," the little owl yawned. "Can we stay in our tree and count the stars until morning?"

The mommy owl smiled and shook her head. "Not tonight, my love. It's time you learned to fly."

"But I'm not good at flying!"
the little owl grumbled.

"Not yet," said his mom. "But you will be if
you try. Look!" Then she spread her strong,
beautiful feathers and leaped from the tree.

"I have scary rumbles in my tummy!" the little owl said.

"Don't let that stop you!" called his mom.

So he shuffled
along the branch,

opened his wings,

closed his eyes,   and dropped

like a rock.

"Good try!" said the mommy owl.
"You were very brave."

"But I did it all wrong," he sighed.

"Yes. But how else will you learn to do it right? If you dare to fall, and fall and fall again, then one day, you will fly."